DIRTY MONEY

Mel Cebulash

NEW READERS PRESS

Copyright © 1993
New Readers Press
Publishing Division of Laubach Literacy International
Box 131, Syracuse, New York 13210-0131

All rights reserved. No part of this book may be
reproduced or transmitted in any form or by any
means, electronic or mechanical, including
photocopying, recording, or by any information
storage and retrieval system, without permission
in writing from the publisher.
Printed in the United States of America

Illustrated by Bill Baylis

9 8 7 6 5 4 3 2

Library of Congress Cataloging-in-Publication Data
Cebulash, Mel
Dirty money : a Sully Gomez mystery / Mel Cebulash
p. cm.
ISBN 1-56420-002-7
1. Gomez, Sully (Fictitious character)—Fiction.
2. Private investigators—California—Los Angeles—
Fiction. 3. Los Angeles (Calif.)—Fiction. 4. Readers
for new literates. I. Title.
[PS3553.E24D57 1993]
813' .54—dc20   93-29071
                                                CIP

 This book was printed on 100% recycled paper,
which contains 50% postconsumer waste.

For Dolly

CHAPTER ONE

The young woman walked right into my office. She handed me a business card. The card read:

> FOR A-1 CLEANING
> Call LaTosha Wilson
> (818) 555-8041

I smiled at the woman and held out the card. "I'm sorry," I said. "I can't use a cleaning service for this small office."

The young woman smiled back at me. "I didn't come here looking for work, Mr. Gomez," she said. "I may need your services. I'm LaTosha Wilson. A-1 Cleaning is my company."

I apologized and slipped her card into my pocket. Then I offered her a seat. "Now

5

tell me why you think you might need a detective, Ms. Wilson," I said. "And please call me Sully. It's short for Sullivan, the name my mother stuck me with."

"Okay," she said, "if you'll call me LaTosha."

I nodded, and she started her story. Five years ago, she had been out of school and out of work. So LaTosha went around to offices in central Los Angeles and asked if she could do some cleaning. LaTosha's friends thought she was crazy, but some kind people offered her a job.

LaTosha did good work, and one job led to another. After a while, she hired others to help her. In no time at all, LaTosha's cleaning work grew into the company she named A-1 Cleaning.

"So what's your problem, LaTosha?" I asked.

"Robbery, I think," LaTosha answered. "Money was taken from one of the offices we clean. The man at that office called me and said he wants his money back."

"That's theft, not robbery," I said. "Did the police tell the man to call you?"

"No," LaTosha said, "the man didn't report the theft. He just wants his money back—no questions asked and no police."

"Do you know who took the money?" I asked.

"I'm not sure," LaTosha said. "Anna Santiago is the woman I had cleaning his office. Anna has been working for me for over two years. So I don't want to believe she took the money."

"By the way," I asked, "how much money are we talking about?"

"The man said $5,000 is missing," LaTosha answered. "I didn't bother calling my insurance company. They would want me to call the police. I don't know what to do. I don't have the $5,000 to hand over to this man."

"Did you think about going to Anna and telling her about the missing money?" I asked. "That's not the same as saying she took it."

"I thought of that," LaTosha said sadly. "The man called me three days ago. I decided to talk to Anna the very next day, except she didn't come to work. She was missing today, too. And she hasn't called. I guess she's not coming back."

LaTosha had a big problem, but I wasn't sure I could help her. "Listen," I said, "even if I find this Anna, she probably won't have much of the money left. You can have her put in jail. Still, if the money is gone, you may never get it back. So what do you think I can do for you?"

LaTosha had no idea. Her eyes filled with tears, and she turned away for a moment. Then she said, "I just don't want to lose my business. If the other people I clean for find out about this theft, they may get scared off. Or they may want me to get a lot more insurance. Ida Walker told me to see you. She said you'd know how to help me."

Ida Walker was an old friend of mine. She probably figured I'd feel sorry for LaTosha. I did feel sorry for her. Still, helping her was another thing. I'd learned long ago that what seem to be simple problems aren't always simple. While LaTosha blew her nose and wiped at her eyes, I thought about her problem. Then I

asked, "The man whose money is missing—what business is he in?"

"I'm not sure," LaTosha said. "I think it has something to do with horses and the racetrack."

I got up. My bad leg was hurting. I'd been sitting too long. I limped around to the front of my desk. "I hurt my leg when I was in the army," I told LaTosha. "I probably can track down this Anna Santiago, but I can't run after her."

"Ida told me about your leg," LaTosha said.

"Okay," I said, "I'll try for a couple of days. I may not be able to help you at all, but I'll try."

She jumped to her feet and took hold of my hand. "Thanks," she said, "thanks very much! Ida was right about you."

I smiled at the remark. In big, bad L.A., Sully Gomez was known as a nice guy. I just hoped I was also known as a good detective. I stretched my right leg and shook it a little. The leg felt better. "Sit down, LaTosha," I said. "I need to know a few other things before I can get started."

CHAPTER TWO

LaTosha Wilson's business did work in L.A. and also in nearby Glendale. The office of the man who had been stolen from was in Glendale. His name was Lester Kelly.

Kelly's office was above a store on Brand Boulevard in Glendale. A-1 Cleaning cleaned Kelly's office and the three other offices on the floor. Until a few days ago, Anna Santiago was the person cleaning the four offices.

I found Kelly's name in the white pages of the phone book. The listing was for his office address. It said "business," but that was all.

After LaTosha left, I tried Kelly's number hoping to find out something about his business. Instead, I got a recorded message telling me Lester Kelly was out. I didn't bother to leave him a message.

It was almost four in the afternoon. I decided to close the office and head for Glendale.

From my office, the drive to Glendale was a short one. Still, it was rush hour. So the traffic on the city streets was heavy. I drove north on Vermont Avenue. At Los Feliz, I turned right. I passed a "Welcome to Glendale" sign minutes later.

Downtown Brand Boulevard is dotted with stores, restaurants, and a few bars. When I got close to the office address, I parked.

Lester Kelly's office was above Pic-Well Men's Clothing Store. A flight of stairs alongside the store led to the four offices.

I checked the office listings at the bottom of the stairs—a lawyer, two insurance agents, and Lester Kelly. Whatever Kelly did, he wasn't telling the world about it.

Instead of going up to Kelly's office, I walked down the street. I wasn't far from a friend's favorite hangout. That friend, Vinnie Cafaro, knew his way around Glendale. Maybe he knew something about Lester Kelly.

The poolroom on Brand is huge. It has about 60 pool tables. They weren't all in use, but it was early.

The players came in all sizes and shapes. Guys in suits were shooting pool. Young women in shorts were shooting pool. Men who looked like pool players were shooting pool. The music was blasting. Basketball players raced across the giant TV screens.

I finally spotted Vinnie Cafaro. He was playing against another guy on a table in the rear. They were playing eight ball.

Vinnie was getting ready to shoot when I reached the table. He nodded at me. From the serious look on Vinnie's face, I knew they weren't playing for fun.

As I watched, Vinnie dropped one striped ball after another. Then he called the eight ball on a bank shot into the side pocket. The ball went in like it was on a string.

The guy playing Vinnie looked sick. "Another game, Bobby?" Vinnie asked.

"No," Bobby said, pulling a handful of money from his pocket.

As I watched, Bobby counted off three $100 bills and gave them to Vinnie. "Later," Bobby said.

"Yeah," Vinnie said, "later."

Bobby walked off, while Vinnie put away his winnings and grinned at me.

"You still have a tough life," I joked.

"I really do," Vinnie said. "You just came at the wrong time. I usually lose."

I knew better, but I wasn't there to talk about his pool shooting. "Do you know anything about a Lester Kelly?" I asked.

Vinnie's eyes darkened. "I know you should stay away from him," Vinnie said.

"He's no good in every way. He's the kind of guy who would enjoy working on your good leg, Sully."

I understood what Vinnie meant, and I figured one limp was all I needed. Still, I had a job to do. If Kelly meant trouble for me, I could imagine how much trouble he would be for LaTosha Wilson.

"Someone supposedly took some big bucks from Kelly's office," I said. "I got tapped to help get the money back to Kelly. So he might be glad to see me."

"He might," Vinnie agreed. "Are the police in on this?"

"No," I said. "How'd you guess?"

Vinnie finished breaking down his pool stick. He slid the three pieces into a carrying case. "We need to talk," he said. "So let's get coffee."

"Sure," I said, wishing Vinnie didn't look so concerned.

CHAPTER THREE

"Kelly doesn't have any real business," Vinnie told me. "I hear he lives in that office. The couch turns into a bed, and the washroom has a shower in it."

"So how does he get money to pay the rent?" I asked.

"Beating on people is one way," Vinnie said. "Kelly is mean and tough. People pay him to work over other people. Oh, the police have a good idea about Kelly, but they need someone to talk. The people hurt by Kelly are afraid to talk. They're scared of him."

"He must have to beat on a lot of people for his rent," I said.

"Oh, Kelly does other things," Vinnie said. "He goes out to the racetrack a lot. He doesn't go to bet or look at the horses. Kelly collects money from gamblers who borrowed it from loan sharks. When the gamblers fall behind in their payments, Kelly shows up."

"What else?" I asked.

Vinnie thought for a moment. "I also heard a rumor that Kelly might be sneaking people into the country," he said.

"The woman who hired me said Kelly just wants his money back," I told Vinnie.

"She didn't say he was mean or anything like that."

"Snakes don't bite all the time," Vinnie said. "If the woman doesn't come up with the money, Kelly will start biting. You can bet on that."

"I'll talk to Kelly," I said. "I'll even try to help him get his money. But I'm not going to let him hurt anybody."

"Just make sure he doesn't hurt you," Vinnie warned. "By the way, I understand he carries a knife all the time."

"Thanks," I said, "I'll watch out for it."

Walking over to Kelly's office, I thought about how he'd been robbed. It was likely a guy like Kelly might have a lot of cash in his office. It wasn't likely he'd have it out in the open. After all, he didn't do business with honest people. So if Anna Santiago took the money, she probably had to search for it. If so, why did she think he'd have a lot of money in his office? Or did she know him for some reason?

I stopped by a pay phone near Kelly's office and called LaTosha Wilson.

"I was just going out," LaTosha said. "What's up?"

"I'm going to see Kelly now," I told her. "I just need to know one thing. How long has Anna Santiago been in this country?"

LaTosha laughed. "Gomez, shame on you!" she said. "Anna was born here. Does that surprise you?"

I laughed back. "Not really," I said, "but it's good news. I didn't want to find out Kelly helped Anna get into the country."

"Is that what he does?" LaTosha asked.

"Along with other nice things," I said. "I'll talk to you tomorrow."

"Okay," LaTosha said, "but be careful."

I told her I would and hung up. The woman who had taken Anna Santiago's place was the one who had to be careful. Cleaning Kelly's office sounded like a dangerous job.

CHAPTER FOUR

I pushed open the door of Lester Kelly's office. A red-haired man was on the phone. Vinnie had told me Kelly's hair was red, so I figured the guy on the phone must be Lester.

"What do you want?" he asked, as soon as he put down the phone.

"Lester Kelly," I said.

"I'm Lester Kelly," he said. "What can I do for you?"

I handed him one of my cards. "I'm working for LaTosha Wilson, the owner of A-1 Cleaning," I said. "I need to know a few things about the missing money."

Lester crushed my card and tossed it into his wastebasket. Obviously, he didn't like detectives any more than he liked cops. "You don't need to talk to me," he said. "You need to talk to the woman who took my money. Or you need to tell Miss A-1 Cleaning to come up with the money while she still can walk around."

Vinnie had been right. Kelly was a snake getting ready to bite. I wasn't about to let him bite LaTosha. He stared hard at me.

"Ms. Wilson hired me to get this matter straightened out," I said. "She told me you had $5,000 stolen. Is that right?"

"Yeah," Kelly said. "I had the money, fifties and hundreds, in an envelope taped underneath the bottom drawer of this desk. The Mexican who cleaned this place took it. Get the picture?"

I didn't like his tone. "Mexican?" I asked. "What makes you think she's Mexican?"

Kelly sneered. "Hey, pal," he said, "I don't care what she is. Just get on my money, not my back!"

I looked around the office. A blanket showed under the pillows on the couch. There were two filing cabinets without labels on them. I figured they were filled

21

with Kelly's socks and underwear. His clothes were probably in the small closet behind his desk.

"Maybe the police need to look into this matter," I said.

Kelly jumped up and stepped around the desk. I watched his hands. If he reached for anything, he was in trouble. Instead, he said, "I told that Wilson woman I didn't want any cops in on this. If the cops show up here, I don't know anything about any missing money. Understand?"

"Sure," I said, "and if we can't get the money, we don't know anything about it. Understand?"

Kelly understood, all right. Still he didn't like what he'd been told. Lester was used to pushing people around. I just figured to be more trouble than most of them. "Okay," he said, controlling his anger. "You do what you can. If you have no luck in finding the cleaning woman, maybe I'll try my luck."

I didn't bother to answer. I didn't know Anna Santiago, and she seemed to have caused the problem. Still I hoped I could find her. If Lester Kelly found her, the money wouldn't be enough. He'd hurt her. He was the type.

I left the office. Behind me, I heard Kelly snap the lock shut. He didn't like me. I smiled at the thought.

Outside, I checked my watch. It was past seven o'clock. The smoggy air smelled good. I felt hungry, but dinner could wait. First, I needed to get out to Anna Santiago's neighborhood. I didn't really expect to find her there, though.

CHAPTER FIVE

Anna Santiago lived on Vermont Avenue. The neighborhood was near Los Angeles City College. The people who lived in the neighborhood were poor.

As I drove, I thought about my talk with Kelly. One thing stuck in my head. L.A. was filled with Spanish-speaking people with Spanish-sounding names. Many people living in L.A. came from Mexico. Yet many others came from Central America, South America, even Cuba. So why had Kelly called Anna Santiago a Mexican? Was his remark another example of his stupidity? Or did he have a reason to think Anna was Mexican?

The number on an old apartment building matched the number of the address LaTosha had given me. Anna was supposed to be around 20 years old. She lived with her mother. LaTosha also thought Anna had a younger brother living at home.

I parked about a block away and walked. I wanted to keep the make of my car a secret. I didn't really think I'd be following anyone, but I've had stranger things happen on cases.

The neighborhood had many people from Spanish-speaking countries. The signs in the store windows told me that. There were other signs in what I guessed was Korean. A few signs were in English.

I counted the doorbells. Anna's building had eight apartments, and a good lock on the front door. Four of the doorbells had names taped above them. Santiago was one of the names.

A minute after I rang the bell, I heard someone coming toward the door. It opened slightly, and a young guy about 14 years old looked out at me. "Can I help you?" he asked.

25

"I'm looking for Anna Santiago," I said.

"There's no Anna here," he said.

He wasn't used to lying. In fact, he seemed sorry he'd tried. "She's not here anymore," he added, looking as if he were about to close the door.

I pushed my way in. The young guy raised his hands like a fighter. I could tell he knew more about fighting than he did about lying. "Hold on," I said. "I'm on Anna's side."

He relaxed a little. I gave him one of my business cards and told him I was working for Anna's boss. "Ms. Wilson is worried about Anna," I said. "She hasn't come to work in a few days. Is Anna all right?"

The young guy wanted to believe me. Finally, he put out his hand and said, "I'm Michael Santiago, Anna's brother."

After we shook hands, I asked, "Where is your sister?"

"She had to go away for a while," he said. "She should have called her boss, but she didn't have time. I know she's sorry about that."

"Is she sorry about the money?" I asked, catching him off guard.

Michael looked sad. "I don't think so," he said. "She's sorry about her job—not the money. The man who had it is a crook." I started to ask him another question. Then I stopped. Michael didn't need any part in this. "Did she tell you what the crook looks like?" I asked.

"Yes," Michael said. "If you looked like him, I wouldn't have opened the door."

"Just you and your mother are here?" I asked.

He nodded.

"If the crook does get into this building, you call the police," I said. "Tell them it's an emergency—a matter of life and death. Do that right away! The guy wants his money, and he is dangerous. So don't be a hero!"

Michael nodded again. I felt sorry for him. He was a young guy. He probably didn't like hanging around. Still, he was trying to protect his mother.

I started to turn for the door. "Wait!" Michael said, grabbing my arm.

"What's the matter?" I asked.

"Can you help Anna?" Michael asked.

"I don't know," I said, "but I'll try. Where is she?"

Michael pulled my card from his pocket and looked at it. "I'll call you," he said. "I need to talk to her first."

"You do that," I said. "Only tell her to call me, and soon!"

Michael nodded. He was worried about his sister. He had a good reason to worry about her. Stealing was never a good idea.

Stealing from Lester Kelly seemed like a very bad idea.

I started out the door. "Hey!" I said, turning back to Michael. "I'm taking your name off the bell."

"Okay," Michael said, but he couldn't hide his anger.

CHAPTER SIX

The next morning, I stopped for a big breakfast at a McDonald's near my office. I figured I was going to need the food for energy. I was right.

My answering machine showed I had two messages. The first message had come in around ten o'clock the night before. It was from Vinnie Cafaro. He wanted me to stop at his "business office" when I had time.

I laughed at Vinnie's message. The poolroom was his business office.

The other message was from LaTosha Wilson. She'd called a few minutes before I got to the office. She wanted me to call as soon as possible.

I looked over the mail. It was garbage. I'd moved to the next level for millions from Publishers Clearing House. I'd also been picked for some fabulous insurance for veterans only. I threw the mail into my wastebasket and called LaTosha Wilson's phone number.

LaTosha answered. She'd gotten a call from Lester Kelly. He'd told LaTosha to forget about finding the money. He'd take care of everything. So LaTosha could call off her detective. Kelly had even apologized for causing her any expense.

"What did you tell him?" I asked.

"I thanked him for letting me know," LaTosha said. "I also told him I was still concerned about Anna. Of course, Mr. Kelly didn't have anything to say about Anna."

"Of course not," I said. "So I guess I'm off the job. You gave me a few days' pay. I'll send some of the money back."

"What happened at Anna's house?" LaTosha asked.

I went over my short meeting with Michael. Then LaTosha said, "Maybe Anna will call. It sounds as if she needs help. If she calls, maybe you can do something for her. Anyway, use up the time I paid for. Okay?"

"That sounds fair enough to me," I said. "I'll let you know if I hear from her."

After I put down the phone, I felt a little guilty. I knew I should have told LaTosha that I'd already decided to help Anna. Her brother had seemed like a nice, honest kid. I figured Anna was the same kind of person. So I really wanted to hear her story.

I hung around the office for about an hour, hoping for some word from Anna. She didn't call, so I drove back to Glendale. As always, Vinnie was busy teaching some guy how to play pool.

Vinnie smiled at me and speeded up the lesson he was giving. When Vinnie sank the eight ball, his student tossed $20 at him. "You hustled me," the guy said.

"No," Vinnie said, "I just got lucky. Anytime you want a chance to get even, you got it. Except right now, my friend here is waiting to buy me coffee."

"Yeah," the guy said, looking my way. "No problem. I'll catch you again."

The guy tossed the pool stick onto the table and stomped off. Vinnie grinned at me, as he packed up the pool balls. "How do you like that guy?" Vinnie asked. "I even played with a house stick, and he says I hustled him. I don't like sore losers."

"No," I said, laughing, "you just like plain losers."

At the coffee shop, Vinnie turned serious. "I did a little asking around about Kelly," Vinnie said. "He isn't sneaking people into the country. He's just the guy who sets up meetings."

"Go on," I said.

"People already in the country want to bring in some relatives," Vinnie said. "Kelly checks out the people. He finds out if they have enough money to pay for the service. Of course, Kelly gets paid up front before he even does a thing. Then if the people have enough money, Kelly turns them over to the border bandits. They sneak the people in."

"So Kelly's a middleman," I said. "He doesn't make much, and he doesn't risk much."

33

"There's more," Vinnie said. "Kelly hangs onto the people who don't have enough money. Of course, Lester Kelly doesn't tell them that. He just tells them he'll handle everything. Then he sets it up so the people trying to cross the border get nowhere."

"He turns them in?" I asked.

"No," Vinnie answered, "but he maps out an impossible route. He probably even waits for them on this side of the border to make it look good."

"How does he get away with it?" I asked.

Vinnie shook his head in disgust. "Kelly yells at the people who paid him," he said. "He tells them that their relatives didn't follow instructions. Kelly makes the people think he risked his life because of their relatives."

"And they believe it?" I asked.

"Maybe not," Vinnie said, "but what can they do? They can't go to the police. They can't go to the FBI. Some people probably want their money back. They have a better chance of getting their relatives a ride on the president's private jet."

"I think I'm beginning to understand a few things," I said. "Anna Santiago must have found out he was taking money from people who were trying to help their relatives."

"Yeah," Vinnie agreed, "and she might have found some of it in his office when she was cleaning. That makes sense."

"But what made her think she could take it?" I asked.

Vinnie shook his head. "That's the $5,000 question," he said, "and I'll bet Kelly knows the answer."

"So does Anna," I said, looking at my watch. "I left word for her to call me at my office. I think I'd better get back there."

I got up and started for the door. My bad leg felt a little stiff. "Watch out for Lester," Vinnie called after me.

At the moment, my mind was on the stiffness in my leg. I should have been thinking about Kelly.

CHAPTER SEVEN

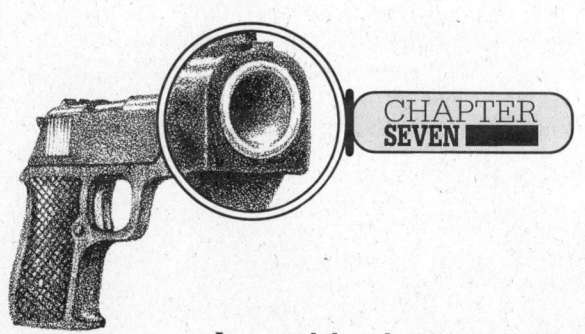

I raced back to my office. As soon as I pushed open the door, I went right over to my desk. The answering machine was blinking. I had three messages.

I reached across the desk and pulled out the center drawer. I was looking for a sheet of paper to write on.

I was hoping one of the messages was from Anna. Just as I found the paper, I realized I wasn't alone. I swung around.

Lester Kelly had been behind the door when I walked into the office. He'd gotten in somehow. He was smiling.

I thought about smiling, too. I couldn't do it. The .32 in Kelly's hand wasn't making me happy.

"What do you want?" I asked.

"Did you talk to the Wilson woman?" Kelly asked.

"Yeah," I said, "I'm off your case, so put away your gun."

"I'll put it away in a while," Kelly said. "First, I want you to do something for me."

"How'd you get in here?" I asked.

Kelly grinned. "Your building manager loved the idea of giving you a surprise," Kelly said. "Me, your old army buddy coming all the way from New York to see you again after all these years. Your manager likes you."

"I like him, too," I said. "I'd rather have him make a mistake than get hurt by one of your kind."

"No one's going to get hurt," Kelly said. "I just want to hear your messages. Then I'll go on my way."

"Didn't you have time to play them?" I asked, wondering if Kelly would be stupid enough to shoot me over the messages.

"I didn't want to make any mistakes with the machine," Kelly said. "Erased messages are no good for anybody. Now, go ahead. Play them back!"

Lester pushed the gun against the side of my head. "I forgot how the machine works," I lied.

I was sorry as soon as the words came out of my mouth. I was dealing with a bad guy with a gun, and I was mouthing off to him. Not smart at all.

On that point, Lester agreed with me. Before I could move, Kelly slammed the gun off the side of my head.

When I woke up, I was on the floor of my office. Kelly was gone, and my head was begging for an aspirin.

I felt my head. The lump was big, but no blood showed on my fingers. I got up slowly and dropped into the chair behind my desk.

My watch showed 4:45. I hadn't been out long. Kelly must have left quickly. Why? The answering machine showed I had no messages. Kelly had figured out how to play the machine. I rewound the tape, hoping he hadn't figured out how to erase the messages.

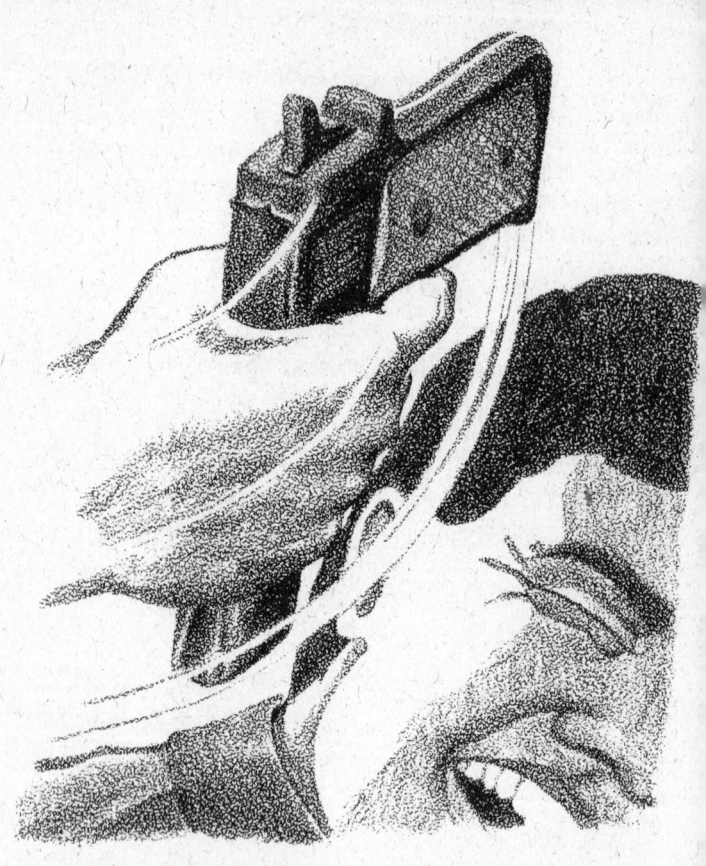

The tape played back loud and clear. The first message was from an insurance agent wanting to show me a wonderful accident policy. As I rubbed my head, I decided she was too late. The second message was from a friend of mine—nothing important.

The third message was the one Kelly wanted. The woman speaking said that she was Anna Santiago. She said she wanted to explain about the money. I was to meet her at a coffee shop on La Brea at five o'clock. She'd be alone in a booth in the rear. If I didn't show by 5:30, she'd call again tomorrow. My head was killing me, but I didn't have time to worry about it. I hoped Anna would spot Kelly's red hair before he spotted her. I also hoped she had the bad habit of not being on time.

CHAPTER EIGHT

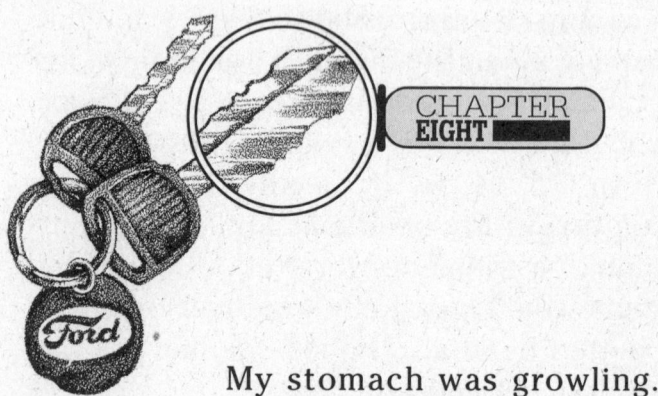

My stomach was growling. On Friday nights, I usually ate at Bona Corso's. It's a little Italian restaurant in Pasadena with good food, good prices, and friendly people. Sometimes I took a date along.

This Friday, I had another date—in L.A., on La Brea. As I drove, the five o'clock news cut off the music on my classic rock radio station. So now I was late.

Minutes later, I pulled into a parking spot near the coffee shop. I hoped I didn't have to use the loaded gun in my jacket.

I guessed Kelly was about six feet tall and 200 pounds. So that gave him a couple of inches and about 30 pounds over me. I wasn't worried about slugging it out with Kelly. He looked flabby. His gun worried me. I knew Kelly was stupid enough to use the gun—and not only as a hammer.

Before I got to the front door of the coffee shop, Lester Kelly walked out. I couldn't miss his red hair. He was holding the arm of a young woman. She looked frightened. I was sure she was Anna Santiago. I ducked behind a car and tried to gather my thoughts.

Kelly moved fast and pulled Anna along with him. I suspected they were going to his car. Trying to jump Kelly seemed like a bad idea. He had a tight hold on Anna. She wasn't going to get away.

Kelly dragged Anna to the driver's side of an old Ford and pulled out some keys. Once the door was open, Kelly pushed Anna into the car and motioned for her to slide to the passenger side.

I rushed back to my car. By the time I got into it, Kelly was pulling away from the curb. I made a quick U-turn and got behind Kelly's car.

I kept as far behind Kelly's car as I could without losing him. I wanted to take him by surprise if I got a chance. Otherwise, I just had to take him. I knew I didn't have much time. Every minute with Kelly probably meant danger for Anna Santiago.

Kelly swung over to Highland Avenue and turned north. I got a little closer, not wanting to lose him because of a red light.

At Melrose, Kelly turned east. If my guess was right, Kelly was headed for the building where Anna lived. Maybe she had the money there. Or maybe he just thought she had the money there.

When Kelly's Ford turned onto Vermont, I was sure he was going to Anna's place. I figured she was safe until they got there.

When Kelly's car reached the building, he braked to a stop. Then he started moving again. He passed the building and turned at the next corner.

I parked and jumped out of my car. I ran to the corner. I could see the glow of Kelly's brake lights down the street. He was parking out of sight.

I needed to move fast. Surprising Kelly from behind a car was a possibility. The danger was in someone on the street jumping into the matter. I didn't want anyone killed—especially someone trying to be a good citizen.

I raced back to the building and pushed the bell—the one I'd pulled the tape off. Michael, be home, I said to myself. Be home and get down here fast!

CHAPTER NINE

I looked out the front door. Kelly and Anna hadn't turned the corner yet. I still had time, but I didn't imagine I had much time. So I pushed the bell again.

Seconds later, the door opened. Michael smiled at me. "Did you see . . . ?" he started to say.

"No time to talk," I said, stepping inside and closing the door. "Is your mother home?"

"No," he said. "Why?"

"Move!" I said, giving him a little push. "Your sister's coming with the guy you told me was a crook. When they walk into your apartment, I want to be waiting for them."

46

"Me, too," he said, moving faster.

"No," I said, "you'll be waiting down the hall. If you hear a gun shot or some other noise, go to a neighbor's apartment and call the police."

"My sister," he said. "She needs me."

"Anna needs you to do what I just told you," I said.

The Santiago apartment was on the second floor. Michael opened the door. "Maybe I should stay with you," he said.

I didn't have time to discuss the matter with him. So I pulled the gun from my jacket. His eyes opened wide. "Go up to the third floor," I said. "Keep out of sight and listen. If you hear any trouble, get help. Now get going, Michael!"

My gun got Michael Santiago's attention. All of a sudden, his sister's troubles seemed bigger than he'd imagined. Talk of a shot is one thing. The sight of a gun is another. Michael decided he could help Anna by following my directions.

I watched Michael go up the stairs. Then I closed the door to the Santiago apartment and looked around. Kelly was going to get the surprise of his ugly life.

Minutes later, I heard footsteps in the hall. "You promised to leave my brother alone," Anna cried.

"Hey," Kelly said, "you just get this door open and get my money. What happens to your brother is up to you."

"But I don't have . . . ," Anna started to say.

Kelly pushed her against the door. "Give me those keys," he said.

Anna didn't hit the door hard, but I held my breath. I hoped Michael didn't panic and run for help. If he did, his sister might end up dead.

After seconds that seemed like hours, the door swung open. "Get in there," Kelly said, pushing Anna into the apartment.

"Michael," Anna asked in a whisper, "where are you?"

Kelly stepped in behind Anna. He had a strong hold on her arm.

I rammed my gun under Kelly's chin and gave him a good look at me. "Turn her loose," I said.

Kelly released Anna, and she looked puzzled. "I'm Sully Gomez," I told her. "Sorry I missed you at the coffee shop."

"Oh," Anna said, still looking puzzled.

"Listen," I said, "I'll explain everything in a minute. Just get Mr. Kelly's gun—and I think he has a knife. Get that, too. Put them in the sink. Then we can talk."

"She stole my money," Kelly said, as Anna started searching him.

I grabbed his red hair and pressed the gun to his neck. "You forgot that I owe you

49

one," I said. "Make one more move, and you'll be living on aspirins for the rest of your life."

Kelly settled down. He wasn't looking for a headache. Anna found his knife. She put it and his gun in the sink. As she did, I let go of Kelly's hair and moved him into a chair by the kitchen table.

"Your brother is fine," I told Anna. "He's upstairs waiting for me."

Anna brightened up. "I was so worried about Michael," she said. "He had nothing to do with this. I didn't want anything to happen to him."

"No one is going to get hurt," I said. "Now go over there and call the police. Mr. Kelly can tell them about his troubles. And about his gun and knife."

The brightness in Anna Santiago's eyes disappeared. Fear took over. "No," she said, "we can't call the police!"

CHAPTER TEN

I figured the stolen money had Anna worried. I also figured her explanation would be better than anything Kelly could say.

"I think we'll have to call the police," I told Anna. "First, I want you to go upstairs and tell Michael everything is all right. Don't bring him back here. Send him on his way. Your brother doesn't need to be in on this."

Anna nodded and left the apartment. "I hope that gun belongs to you," I said to Kelly.

"You heard the woman," Kelly said. "The police don't fit in this. It's a private matter between me and Anna."

I didn't bother to answer. I felt like giving Lester Kelly a private headache, but there was no sense in hitting him. So I waited for Anna. From the time she took, I gathered Michael still had trouble listening.

As soon as Anna came back into the apartment, I walked over to the phone on the kitchen wall. "Now tell me why I shouldn't call the police," I said, "and talk fast. Mr. Kelly is getting tired of waiting."

"I cleaned his office all the time," Anna said, pointing at Kelly. "Sometimes he was there while I was cleaning because he lives in his office. Anyway, he started telling me that he helped a lot of people get into the country."

"Why did he tell you?" I asked.

"Mr. Kelly thought I was Mexican," Anna said, grinning slightly. "He was a little disappointed when I told him I was born in L.A."

"Go on," I said.

"I told some of my friends about Kelly," Anna said. "One friend was from Guatemala. He had relatives who wanted to get into the U.S."

"So you asked Mr. Kelly," I said.

"Right!" she said. "To make a long story short, Mr. Kelly agreed to help my friend's relatives for $5,000. My friend paid the money, but no one helped his relatives. Mr. Kelly blamed the relatives. He said they'd been talking too much and messed up the deal. The people across the border who were supposed to help got angry and just kept the money. That was it. My friend's money was gone."

"Of course, he couldn't go to the police," I said. "You can't complain to the law when you're breaking it."

"I know," Anna agreed.

"So where do you fit with the $5,000?" I asked.

"A few days after that, I was cleaning Mr. Kelly's office," Anna said. "He'd been drinking a lot. He thanked me for getting him the $5,000 job. He said he liked nice, easy jobs like that."

"In other words," I said, "he was telling you he didn't do a thing for the guy."

"Yeah," Anna said, "and he gave me a $50 bill from an envelope under his desk.

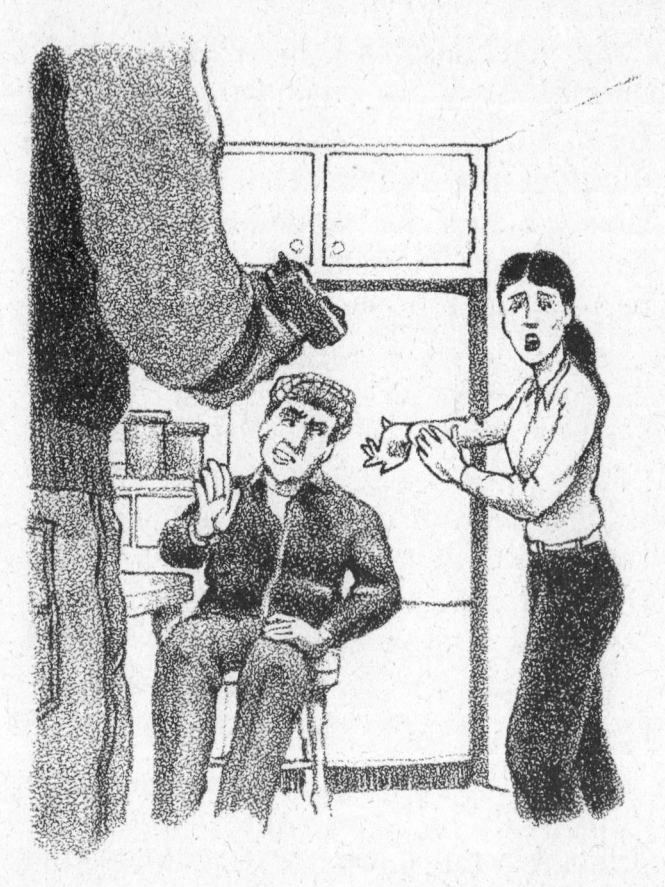

He called it a fee for finding the customer. He said I should try to find him more customers."

"Did you?" I asked.

"No," Anna said, "I came back to the office later that night. Kelly wasn't around.

I took $5,000 from the envelope taped underneath the bottom drawer of his desk. There was more money than that, but I only took the $5,000. I gave it back to my friend."

"You what?" Kelly asked.

"I gave it back to my friend," Anna said. "I was afraid to tell you."

Kelly shook his head in disgust. "You'll be cleaning offices forever," he said to Anna.

"You shut your mouth," I told Kelly.

Kelly shut up, and I stood there looking at Anna. I could understand why she didn't want to go to the police. The law didn't give people a right to steal, even from thieves. Anna knew that now. She'd learned some hard lessons. Don't steal from thieves and don't deal with them. The lessons were good ones.

Finally I said, "Let's go, Kelly."

"Where are we going?" Kelly asked, sounding nervous.

"For a little ride," I said, poking him with my gun to get him moving. "Just you and me. My car is parked out front. When we get out there, don't get any smart ideas. In this neighborhood, people have the bad habit of minding their own business."

CHAPTER ELEVEN

Anna Santiago was a nice young woman. She was worried about Lester Kelly. I could see the fear in her eyes. She'd watched too many movies on TV. She thought I was going to kill the man.

"Don't go anywhere," I said to Anna. "I'll be back."

As Kelly and I went down the stairs, I hoped I could make him as nervous as Anna was.

Going to the police was out. Kelly would say he had no money. Anna's friend would say he'd never paid anyone any money. The police had real crimes to worry about. This case was a crime that didn't happen.

It was "all's well that ends well"—except for Lester Kelly.

Outside, I opened my car on the driver's side and let Kelly slide into the passenger seat. I got in and stared over at Lester. He didn't look happy at all.

"I don't suppose a lot of people are going to miss you," I said.

"What do you mean?" Kelly asked.

"I mean if you were missing," I said. "Would anybody ask the police to look for you?"

"Hey," Kelly said, "I'm not out of money. I lost the $5,000. So what? I have other money. I'll pay you to forget about the whole thing. You can use some money. I'm sure the woman with the cleaning company isn't paying you much. She sure isn't paying you for what you're thinking about."

"I'm Sully Gomez," I said. "Did you forget that? There are lots of Gomezes. Some are on the other side of the border. Did you ever cheat a Gomez? Did you tell him you'd get his relatives into the country?"

Kelly was sweating. "No," he said, "I never made any deals with any Gomez. I swear I didn't."

"I don't believe you," I said, and started the car engine.

Kelly started to reach for my arm, and then changed his mind. "Hold on," he pleaded. "The guy got his money back. I don't care about it. I won't bother that Anna ever again. I won't even talk to her when she cleans my office. You can check with her. Isn't that enough?"

"Almost," I said. "In fact, I think we might be able to make a deal."

"How?" Kelly asked.

I outlined my plan to him. He had a month to move. During that time, he'd clean his own office. He could go wherever he wanted.

"You stay away from LaTosha Wilson and Anna Santiago," I warned Kelly. "If either one of them has any problem with you, you're back to having a problem with me. Remember, I still owe you one."

"No trouble," Kelly said, "and no problems."

I didn't trust him, except he had no reason to bother LaTosha or Anna. The $5,000 was gone. "I hope the cops get you one of these days," I said. "Until then, stay out of my way. Now get lost."

Kelly reached for the door handle. "What about my gun and . . . ?" he started to say.

I cut him off. "You didn't learn a thing, did you?" I asked.

Kelly decided he should go. Without another word, he got out of the car and went off down the street. I watched him until he turned the corner. He didn't look back. I expected that LaTosha, Anna, and I had seen the last of Lester Kelly.

CHAPTER TWELVE

I climbed out of my car. As I locked it, I spotted Michael Santiago in a doorway across the street. I think he thought he was hiding. I waved for him to cross over.

"I was waiting for Anna," Michael said.
"You don't have to wait anymore," I said. "You can go home. Come on."

Upstairs, I told Anna what had happened with Kelly. "You call me if he ever bothers you," I said. "I don't think he will."

"I don't think I'll see him again," Anna said. "LaTosha doesn't want me to work for her anymore."

61

"No," I said, "I guess not. She has to have people she can trust. She can't spend her time watching the people who work for her."

"She never had to watch me," Anna said, but her heart wasn't in the words. She knew she'd made a mistake—with Kelly and her job.

* * *

About two months later, I had lunch with LaTosha Wilson. I liked her, and I wanted to be sure Kelly hadn't bothered her after his move.

"An employment service moved into Kelly's office," LaTosha said. "A man runs the service, but he doesn't live in the office."

"That's good," I said. "I'm sure the office is easier to clean."

"I think so," LaTosha said. "By the way, Anna is starting back to work next week. She made a mistake, but we all do."

"Right," I said, smiling, "and Anna is lucky she has a soft-hearted boss."

LaTosha smiled back. "Michael is the lucky one," she said. "When I called Anna, Michael answered the phone. He told me about the nice guy who took him to a Lakers game—the detective."

"Don't spread that story around," I said, grinning. "It's not good for my business."